# HOW TO TRICK OR TREAT IN OUTER SPACE

by

KATHLEEN KRULL

illustrated by

PAUL BREWER

Holiday House / New York

to Gerry Fialka and Suzy Williams,
for their early encouragement

Text copyright © 2004 by Kathleen Krull
Illustrations copyright © 2004 by Paul Brewer
All Rights Reserved
Printed in the United States of America
www.holidayhouse.com
First Edition
1 3 5 7 9 10 8 6 4 2

Library of Congress Cataloging-in-Publication Data

Krull, Kathleen.
How to trick or treat in outer space / by Kathleen Krull ;
illustrated by Paul Brewer.—1st ed.
p. cm.
Summary: Three extraterrestrial brothers go trick-or-treating
on various planets.
ISBN 0-8234-1844-8 (hardcover)
[1. Halloween—Fiction. 2. Extraterrestrial beings—Fiction.
3. Brothers—Fiction.] I. Brewer, Paul, 1950- ill. II. Title.

PZ7.K9418Ho 2004
[E]—dc22
2003068599

You think earthlings are the only

It's the biggest night of

the year in outer space!

First stop, the Pumpkin planets. Not too scary.

On planet Suzy, everyone looks like . . . . Suzy!

Goofy tricks on Pluto.

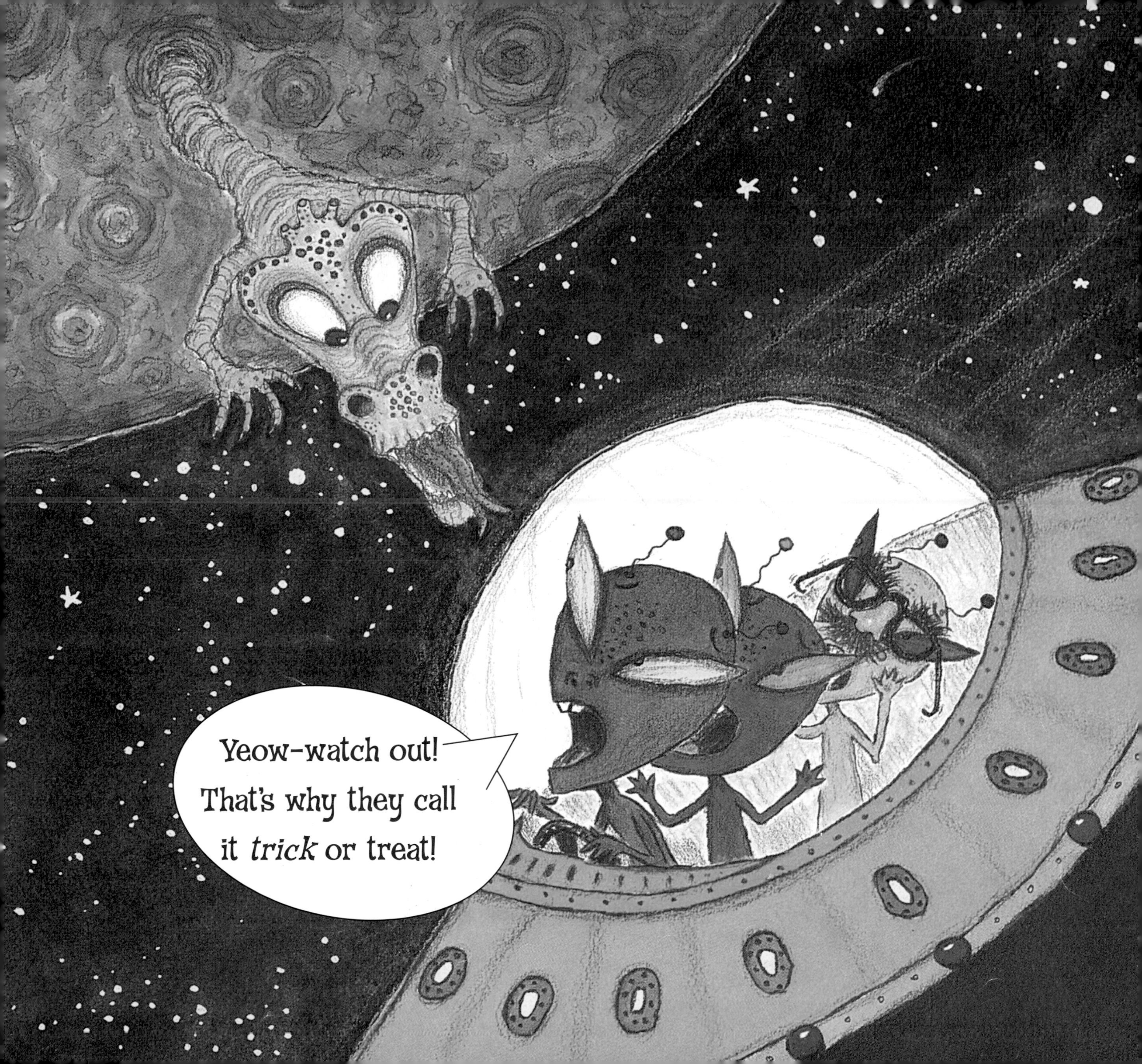
Yeow–watch out! That's why they call it *trick* or treat!

Guess what lives on Jupiter?
Big giant robots.

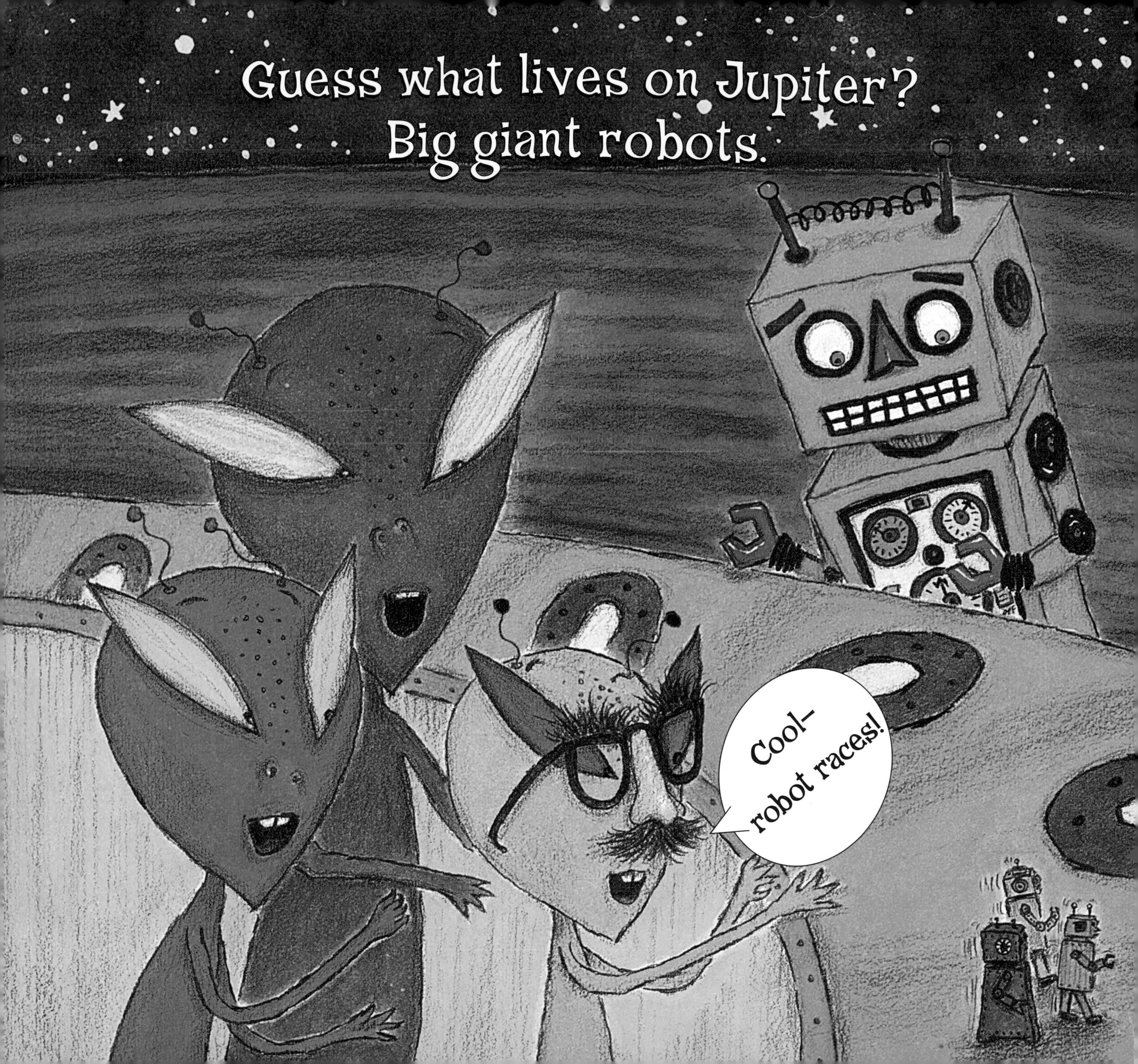

Next stop, Mars.

Whew, that was close!

But now we're *LOST*!

Didn't we pass Pluto?
I think we passed Pluto a light-year ago.
No, no. I see where we are. Just turn left here and it's not far at all!
Map of the UNIVERSE
SO LET'S GO HOME!

So, Da Moon, what did you think of Halloween?
WOWIE ZOWIE! Let's do it again tomorrow!